**JEREMY STRONG** once worked in a bakery, putting the jam into three thousand doughnuts every night. Now he puts the jam in stories instead, which he finds much more exciting. At the age of three, he fell out of a first-floor bedroom window and landed on his head. His mother says that this damaged him for the rest of his life and refuses to take any responsibility. He loves writing stories because he says it is 'the only time you alone have complete control and can make anything happen'. His ambition is to make you laugh (or at least snuffle). Jeremy Strong lives near Bath with his wife, Gillie, four cats and a flying cow.

## ARE YOU FEELING SILLY ENOUGH TO READ MORE?

LAUGH YOUR SOCKS OFF WITH

# JEREMY STRONG

## CARTOON KID ZOMBIES!

ILLUSTRATED BY
**STEVE MAY**

PUFFIN

# PUFFIN BOOKS

Published by the Penguin Group
Penguin Books Ltd, 80 Strand, London WC2R 0RL, England
Penguin Group (USA) Inc., 375 Hudson Street, New York, New York 10014, USA
Penguin Group (Canada), 90 Eglinton Avenue East, Suite 700, Toronto, Ontario, Canada M4P 2Y3
(a division of Pearson Penguin Canada Inc.)
Penguin Ireland, 25 St Stephen's Green, Dublin 2, Ireland (a division of Penguin Books Ltd)
Penguin Group (Australia), 250 Camberwell Road, Camberwell, Victoria 3124, Australia
(a division of Pearson Australia Group Pty Ltd)
Penguin Books India Pvt Ltd, 11 Community Centre, Panchsheel Park, New Delhi – 110 017, India
Penguin Group (NZ), 67 Apollo Drive, Rosedale, North Shore 0632, New Zealand
(a division of Pearson New Zealand Ltd)
Penguin Books (South Africa) (Pty) Ltd, 24 Sturdee Avenue, Rosebank, Johannesburg 2196, South Africa

Penguin Books Ltd, Registered Offices: 80 Strand, London WC2R 0RL, England

puffinbooks.com

First published 2013
001

Text copyright © Jeremy Strong, 2013
Illustrations copyright © Steve May, 2013
All rights reserved

The moral right of the author and illustrator has been asserted

Set in Baskerville
Made and printed in England by Clays Ltd, St Ives plc

British Library Cataloguing in Publication Data
A CIP catalogue record for this book is available from the British Library

ISBN: 978-0-141-34417-1

www.greenpenguin.co.uk

MIX
Paper from
responsible sources
FSC™ C018179
www.fsc.org

Penguin Books is committed to a sustainable
future for our business, our readers and our
planet. This book is made from paper certified
by the Forest Stewardship Council.

ALWAYS LEARNING                    **PEARSON**

*This is for Patric,*
*who tells the best stories*
*and keeps the best B&B in London.*
*Many thanks!*

# CONTENTS

Those are just some of the noises we
make when our teacher makes a special
announcement, like he had just done.

Mr Butternut is brilliant. (Well, most of the
time, anyhow. Sometimes he gets moody or cross
and then he is not so brilliant and I call him

Mr Horrible Hairy Face. That's because he has got a BEARD. Hairy, or what? Hairy, that's what!)

Anyhow, it was Wednesday afternoon at school and Mr Butternut made his announcement.

FRIDAY WILL BE A SHOW AND TELL DAY!

Liam looked completely blank and said to me, 'Casper, what is a *Show and Tell day*?'

Honestly, Liam never understands anything.

BUT HOW CAN YOU **SHOW** A DAY?

My best friend Pete and I call him Captain Weird. That's his superhero name. In fact, we are all superheroes. Mr Butternut told us that when we first became his class.

CARTOON KID!

BIG FEET PETE!

CURLY WURLY GIRLY!

BIG BUM BRAIN!

I am Cartoon Kid because I am always drawing stuff. Pete is Big Feet Pete because he has big feet. Obviously. Then there's Curly-Wurly-Girly, Scaredy Pants, Exploding Girl, Big Bum Brain and all sorts of others. Big Bum Brain is really Sarah Sitterbout. Sarah is rather large, everywhere, ESPECIALLY her brain. She is incredibly clever and quite possibly the most intelligent girl in the school, if not the universe. She knows everything, even how to spell

psychiya, ~~psychiya,~~

~~psykiya,~~

~~sikiya,~~

~~phsychia -~~

# PSYCHIATRIST!

# PHEW!

Anyhow, Liam was waiting for an answer, so I told him.

'We each bring in something to SHOW the class and we TELL everyone why we brought it in. What will you bring in, Liam?'

'I don't know,' he said, which is what he says to most questions.

He's a bit odd, but do you know what? I think that just about everyone is a bit odd in some way, so that being odd must make most of us quite normal. Does that make sense? Probably not. Do we care? No, we don't. Shall I talk about something else? Yes, Casper, get on with it!

SPOT THE ODD ONE OUT

(HA HA HA! THEY'RE ALL ODD!!)

Of course, there was MUCHO excitement about the Show and Tell day at the end of the week. We were all asking each other what we were going to bring in.

Hartley Tartly-Green was almost jumping
out of his trousers. (Jolly good thing he didn't!
That would certainly have been a Show and
Tell day! Ha ha!)

'I'm going to bring my new ebook! No, I'm going to bring my new socks that light up in the dark so you can see where you're putting your feet!'

'And I'm going to bring the biggest cork ever and stick it in your mouth, Hartley,' snapped Noella Niblet, who is always moaning about something. That's why we call her The Incredible Sulk.

'Class! Class! Please!' cried Mr Butternut. 'Quieten down. Noella, that was an unkind thing to say. I'm sure you will all think of something interesting to show the others. If you can't think of anything, come and talk to me about it during the week. I will help you.'

# SOME INTERESTING THINGS

LIGHT-UP SOCKS

PARP!
FART CUSHION

SPIDER CATCHER

CHEESE HAT

Our teacher is like that. Sometimes he brings in things himself and secretly gives them to anyone who has nothing to show. That Mr Butternut is pretty amazing, if you ask me. And he's still pretty amazing even if you DON'T ask.

CAT PANTS

POOPER SCOOPER

Pete and I walked home together after school. That's because we live next door to each other. Plus, we are best friends, as you know.

← BEST FRIENDS! →

'What are you going to take in on Friday, my tiny ginger stick insect?' asked Pete.

He's always calling me things like that because I am short and have knobbly knees and ginger hair. I don't mind him calling me names. That's because I call him Big Nose and Number One Twit Person and so on.

'I don't know. Maybe I could take in my big sis Abbie and show her. Then I could tell everyone how annoying she is and how her brain is missing and stuff like that.'

Pete laughed and said that if I took Abbie in, he would bring Uncle Boring. (Who isn't an uncle, but he is VERY boring. Pete's mum and dad split up three years ago and now his mum has got Uncle Boring as a boyfriend. His real name is Derek.)

Anyhow, we had a good laugh about that all the way home, but by the time we got to our houses we still hadn't actually thought of what we could take in on Friday. It was a bit of a problem.

The next day at school, half the class was talking about what they were going to bring, although it was to be kept secret. Hartley kept banging on about

Surely I'm the Best Thing Ever!

how he was going to bring in the Best Thing Ever, and what was I going to bring in because it couldn't possibly be as good as his because his was the Best Thing Ever and there wasn't anything in the world better than the Best Thing Ever. He went on and on until I thought, *If Hartley Tartly tells me about the*

# B.T.E.

*once more, I shall explode.*

So I told him I was going to bring something
REALLY SPECIAL. (Gulp! It certainly was
special – so special it was INVISIBLE because
it wasn't anything at all!)

That made Hartley think. He turned to Pete
and told him all about the B.T.E. Do you know
what Pete said in reply? It was really cool!

'Well, my thing comes from OUTER
SPACE and it's even better, so there!'

I looked at Pete and wondered what it was he'd thought of to bring in. When we went out for break I asked him. 'What have you got from Outer Space?'

Pete looked at me as if I was completely crackers. 'Nothing! I only said that to shut Hartley up!'

Did I feel like an idiot? Yes, I did, but not for

long because I suddenly realized that we were

being approached by a bunch of zombies.

Actually, it was Masher McNee and his

Monster Mob.

They are Bad News. They are always looking to make trouble, and now it seemed like they planned to make trouble with Pete and me.

Masher rocked up with his arms outstretched and a dead look in his eyes. 'We are zombies!' he cried.

Erin came over to see what was going on. Erin has got knobbly knees like me. Plus, she's got a big black shaggy cat stuck on her head. It's not really a cat – it's just her hair. I don't think Erin knows what a hairbrush is. She certainly hasn't got one. She's a walking mess. She had her jumper on back to front the other day and she didn't even notice.

Anyway, Erin took one look at Masher and said:

DID YOU HAVE MASHED POTATO FOR BREAKFAST?

Masher lowered his arms, utterly puzzled.

Wow! That was pretty brave of her. Nobody, and I mean nobody, tells Masher McNee he looks like mashed potato. Erin hasn't been in our class very long. Maybe she didn't know what Masher was like.

He took a step closer to Erin. 'We are zombies, girly, and YOU had better watch out or I will zombify you!'

'I am SO scared,' said Erin. 'You couldn't zombi*fry* an egg!'

'I said zombiFY, not zombiFRY!' yelled Masher.

Erin folded her arms. 'Do you know what the problem with zombies is? They don't have brains.'

By this time Masher was turning a dull purple colour. 'We're going to get you!' he hissed.

And that was when the whistle blew for the end of breaktime and we all went back into school. Masher looked menacingly at Erin and shook his fist. 'We'll get you!' he yelled.

Pete and I walked back with Erin.

Erin stopped. 'It's what my dad says. When he sees a gang he goes: "Oh, look, it's Sherman and the Sheep."

Dad says kids in gangs are like sheep. They follow one  another round and copy each other, so basically they're just  sheep.' She smiled, pointed at  her head and put on a dopey  voice. 'You know – teeny-weeny brains. *Baaaaaa!*'

 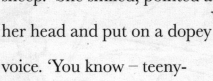 

WOOF!

(BLACK SHEEP OF THE FAMILY!)

And with that she disappeared into class.

Erin's got a really nice smile, and dimples and smudges on her face. At least I think they're smudges. They might be big freckles.

Pete dug his elbow into me. He was grinning and making his eyebrows waggle up and down. 'Casper's in love!' he declared.

'No, I'm not! I think she's brave, that's all.'

'Casper's in – AAARRGGH! OK, I won't say it again.'

STOP STRANGLING ME!

On the way home we chatted about the same
old problem – what to take in for Show and
Tell. We only had one day left to find something.

'Why don't you really take in Uncle Boring?'
I joked.

'Good idea, then he can bore everyone to
death,' Pete nodded. 'And then the police
would arrest him for murder and that would
get rid of him. Job done!'

We had almost reached home when I
spotted a small dark shape lying in the gutter.
We went over and stared at it.

'It's a mouse,' said Pete.

I bent down and shook my head. 'Wow,' I
murmured. 'I think it's a bat. It's a dead bat.'

'Oh, lovely. Can we go home now?'

'Pete, it's a bat! How many times do you see a dead bat – or even an alive bat?'

'Well, actually, my strange twiggy pal, I don't go around looking for them in the first place. Anyhow, you'd better not touch it. You could get some awful disease.'

'I'm not going to touch it, Mr Know-It-All-with-Feet-Like-Skateboards.'

I searched my bag for some paper. In the end I had to tear a page out of my maths book. (I hope Mr Horrible Hairy Face doesn't find out!) I carefully picked up the bat with the paper, wrapped it round and put it in my bag.

'Is that your supper?' asked Pete.

'Of course not. You are Mr Stupido! Tomorrow I shall take it into school for Show and Tell.' I gave Pete a triumphant grin.

'But you can't take a dead bat into school!'

'Why not?' I demanded.

'Because, because, because, because . . .' Pete floundered.

'It'll be really cool,' I suggested.

A smile crept on to Pete's face. 'We found this bat together, didn't we?' he said brightly.

'Um, well, sort of, I suppose.'

'In that case we can both take it in!'

I'm not sure this is a good idea.

'Huh! You are a Crafty Trickster and should be Commander-in-Chief of MI5.'

Pete grinned, gave me a single nod, walked up his path to his front door, shouted 'See you tomorrow, Bat-face!' and went indoors.

That left me with a dead bat in my bag. Hmmm, BIG PROBLEMO. I mean, when things die they start to smell after a while, don't they. I decided that I had better put it in the freezer because that would keep it nice and fresh. So I did.

# SARAH SITTERBOUT'S BIT ABOUT BATS

PRRRRP!

SQUEEAK!

SQUEEAK!

Bats are amazing mammals. Some are as small as mice. The Flying Fox is the largest bat in the world. Most bats eat fruit or insects, but many of the bigger bats eat things like: frogs, small birds, mice and even scorpions. (NOT humans!) Some bats find their way around in the dark by squeaking and using radar, but many bats have excellent eyesight. (Not many people know that!) I like bats, but my dad doesn't because he is a scaredy-wuss.

YUM! YUM!

@#&*

# WAAARRGGHH!

That was the noise my big sis, Abbie, made
when she went to the freezer to get an ice lolly
and instead she got a frozen dead bat. Ha ha!
She went screaming off to tell Mummikins.
And then of course I was in trouble.

So Mum flew off the handle for a bit, but eventually she agreed it could stay in the freezer. 'But only until morning and only if it's in a plastic box with a lid tight shut. Then you can take it into school and after that I never want to see it again,' she added.

Abbie just looked at me as if I was some kind of sluggy-beetley-wormy kind of creature from the Planet Snott.

I CAN'T BELIEVE YOU ARE SO GROSS!

And, to tell you the truth, neither could I. It just seemed like a brilliant idea. I was sure nobody else would be taking a bat into school, dead or alive.

The next morning I got up early and rescued the bat from the freezer. It was really beautiful. The fur was a chocolatey brown, almost black. The wings were so thin you could look through them and see how the bones are just like the ones in our arms and hands. It's amazing!

Pete and I went to school together, with the bat safely sealed up in a plastic bag. The class was very excited and they were all crowding round the door waiting for Mr Butternut to open up for the day.

Hartley Tartly-Green was shouting the loudest, of course. 'It's got over a thousand books in the memory!'

'Pity you can't read, Hartley,' teased Lucy, and several children laughed.

'I can, I *can* read!' Hartley shouted furiously. Of course he could. Everyone knew he could read. The whole class can read.

'What have you brought, Lucy?' asked Pete.

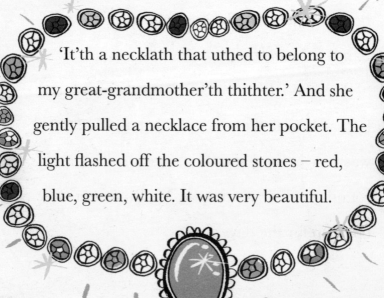

'It'th a necklath that uthed to belong to my great-grandmother'th thithter.' And she gently pulled a necklace from her pocket. The light flashed off the coloured stones – red, blue, green, white. It was very beautiful.

'Those jewels glitter like your teeth!'
Cameron pointed out. It was true. Lucy wears
a metal brace on her teeth. That's why she
can't say the 's' sound properly. Sometimes
her brace flashes in the light. Lucy doesn't like
her brace, but Pete and I call her The Mighty
Munch. When she's a superhero she can eat
ANYTHING with her steel teeth, which
makes her mighty dangerous!

Just then Mr Butternut turned up and let us all into class.

'I see you've all brought something in to show,' he said. 'Let's start with Mia.'

And so we had our Show and Tell day. When it got to my turn I explained that Pete and I had found our special thing together. We stood at the front of the class and I slowly uncovered the plastic bag so everyone could see. Pete gently held one corner and I held the other. We lifted it up in view of the whole class.

'AAARGH!'

'IT'S A-???'

'RUN FOR YOUR LIVES!'

'WAAAHHH!'

The screams! The shouts! Noella and

Cameron both fell off their chairs. Hartley hid

his eyes.

But Mr Butternut beamed the biggest smile you have EVER seen.

'My goodness, you certainly have got something wonderful there,' he told us. 'Well done, boys. That is amazing. Look, you can see the bones in the wings, just like our fingers.'

That teacher of ours is Mr Cool!

Pete and I spent the rest of the day painting pictures of the bat and writing about it and measuring it and finding out all sorts of things about bats. In fact, I am now a bat expert. I bet if you ask me a question about bats, I can tell you the answer. Go on, ask.

**Question:** Why do bats have squashed-up noses?

**Answer:** Not all bats have squashed-up noses. Bats with squashed noses use them to help pick up the sounds they make for echo-location.

**Question:** Doesn't that mean their noses are actually ears?

**Answer:** No, it doesn't! You are Mr Stupido. Stop asking silly questions.

*Huh! Chameleons are much more interesting than bats!*

See – I told you. I know everything (about bats). One day I might even be as clever as Sarah Sitterbout (but not as big).

Anyhow, we had a brilliant day because at lunchtime we went out to play and everybody was talking about the bat. I went back to class and brought it out to show people. And that was just about the time there was a whole pile of screaming going on – and it wasn't about the bat on this occasion. It was Masher McNee and his Monster Mob. They were being zombies again and they were heading our way.

By this time Masher had terrorized about twenty children into being zombies with him, so there was a pretty big gang of them. In fact they looked SCARY SCARY SCARY! (That's three times more than just plain SCARY.)

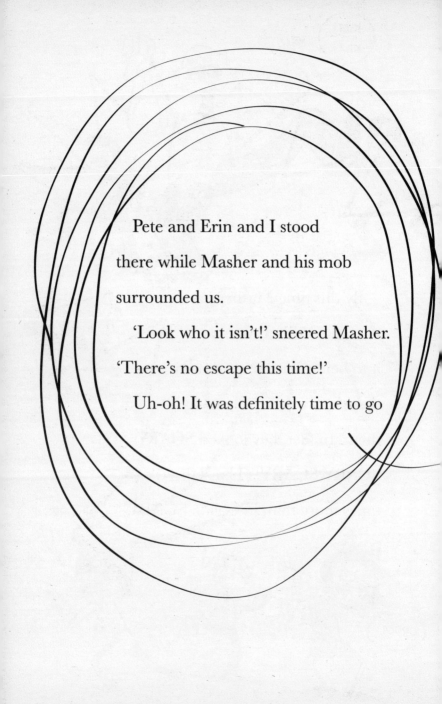

Pete and Erin and I stood
there while Masher and his mob
surrounded us.

'Look who it isn't!' sneered Masher.
'There's no escape this time!'

Uh-oh! It was definitely time to go

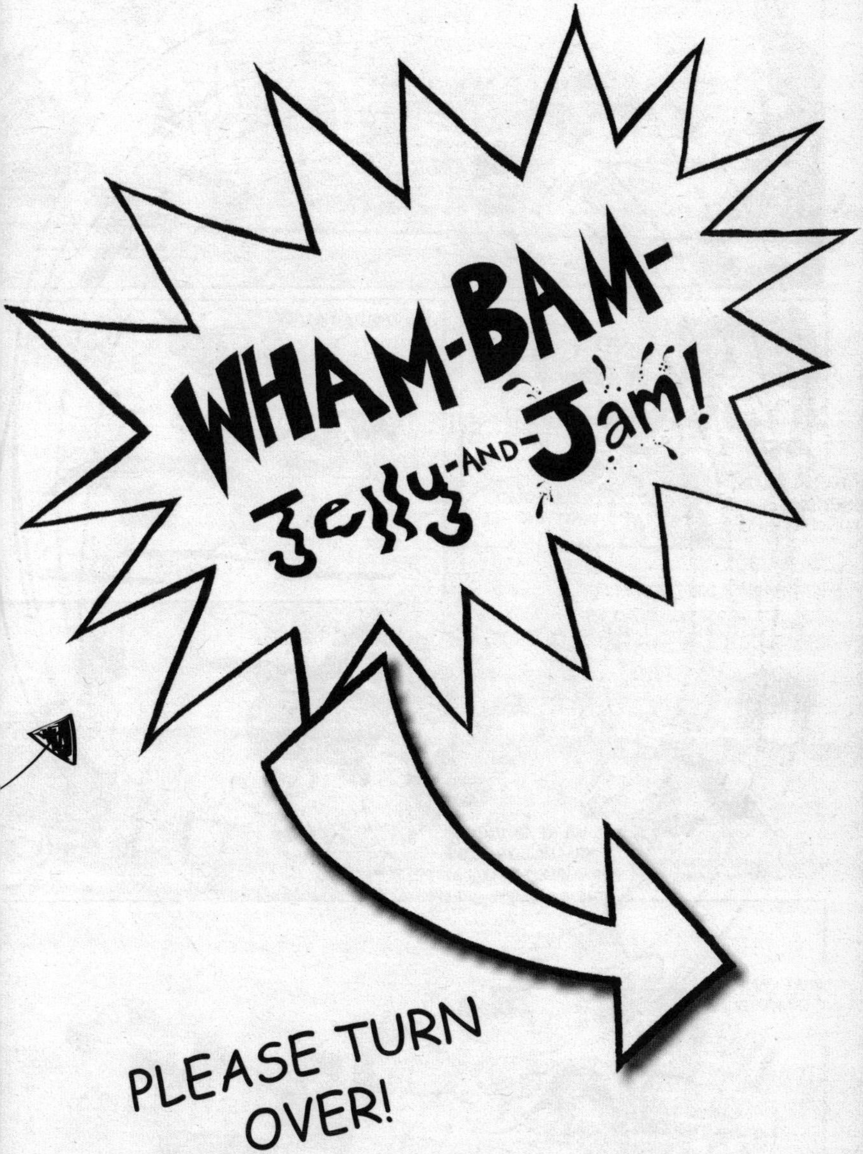


PLEASE TURN OVER!

Do you like mint sauce when you eat lamb for dinner? I do. Yum yum. Unfortunately, Masher wasn't a sheep. I didn't have any mint sauce, either. The zombies were closing in on

us and things were getting very hairy-scary,
eyes-all-starey, when I suddenly remembered
the plastic bag. I held it up, so everyone could
see what was in it.

So that got rid of *them*. Erin was very impressed.

'You saved us! My hero!' she said, and her smile went from one ear to the other.

Meanwhile, I went red from one ear to the other.

ISN'T THAT CUTE?

I scowled at my best friend. 'You are SO dead,' I warned him.

'And you are SO sweet,' tweeted Pete.

'No! NO! I don't want a dead bat down

the back of my neck! Erin, stop him!

Save me! Help! Mummy!'

That'll teach him. Huh!

If you ask me
those children
are completely
BATTY!

# HA! HA! SNIGGER! HA! HA! HA!

That was the noise we ALL made when our head teacher, Miss Scratchitt, introduced the team of inspectors to us at assembly. AAARGH!

INSPECTORS! Exactly. It was very *aaargh!* if you ask me. They looked pretty scary too.

'That one in the middle looks like Mr Potato Head,' muttered Pete, and he was right.

The teachers had been warning us about the inspectors for days and days.

'But what are they going to inspect, Mr Butternut?' asked Sarah Sitterbout when we were back in class.

'Everything,' sighed Mr Butternut.

Liam waved his hand in the air. 'Even our pants?' he asked.

Mr Butternut looked at Liam and groaned. 'No, Liam. Not your pants. Now then, I want to introduce a new boy who is joining our class.'

We all peered round at the new boy. I was thinking how embarrassing it must be to have everyone staring at you. If everyone looked at me, I'd want to hide somewhere.

But the new boy didn't look upset at all. He

grinned back and waved, like the Queen. Well, not the same as the Queen, obviously, because he was a boy and a lot smaller and he wore big spectacles instead of a crown, but you know what I mean.

He grinned and said 'Hi!' in a loud voice.

'This is Sam,' Mr Butternut told us, and Sam grinned even more.

'At my last school they called me Sci-Fi Sam,' he declared. 'That's because I'm going to be a super-scientist when I grow up. I'm going to save the world.'

Mr Butternut smiled and showed all his teeth. (He's got a lot of them. I'm sure he's got twice as many teeth as most people.) 'That's terrific, Sam. I'm sure you will. In any case, we like superheroes in this class, and we are all going to need to be superheroes while the inspectors are here.'

'I could de-materialize them with my anti-matter splatter gun,' Sam piped up.

'Really?' said Mr Butternut.

'Well, I haven't actually made one yet, but I know what it does. It makes people vanish.'

'That sounds very useful.' Our teacher looked thoughtful and I knew exactly what he was thinking.

PIP! POP! GONE!

ANTI-MATTER SPLATTER™

Sam sat at the next table and we soon discovered that he wasn't just good at science. He was also good at talking. He went on and on! We sat there and listened and our eyes got bigger and bigger with the things he was telling us.

'Nothing can travel faster than light. That's because the faster anything goes, the slower it gets . . .'

'Hang on,' Pete interrupted. 'That doesn't make sense.'

'It does,' nodded Sam. 'That's because the faster you travel, the heavier you get, so you slow down. That's why time machines can't really exist.'

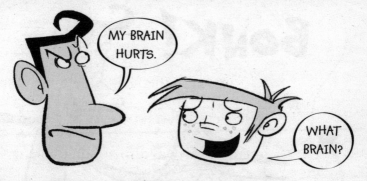

Pete turned to me and gave me a very superior kind of look. 'I will have you know, my tiny ginger nutkin, that my brain won first prize at Britain's Best and Brightest Brain Display only last week. So there.'

'In that case,' I returned, 'you must have been the only contestant. So there back.'

Sam was puzzled. 'Do you two always argue like that?'

'Yes,' I said. 'We're best friends.'

'You sound like best enemies,' Sam observed.

Pete nodded and smiled. 'Exactly. Same thing really.'

Erin tapped Sam's arm. 'Just ignore them. They're crazy.'

# SARAH SITTERBOUT'S BIT ABOUT LIGHT SPEED

Light travels faster than anything else known to man. Its speed is about 186,282 miles per SECOND! That is fast! Stars are so far from Earth that we measure their distance in LIGHT YEARS.

Many stars are so many light years away from Earth that by the time their light reaches us they may not even be there any more. They might have exploded! I wish the school inspectors would explode!

We were just getting our books out when the door opened and in came the round inspector. He nodded at us all and told us to continue with whatever we were doing. So Tyson carried on picking his nose and I carried on falling off my chair. It wasn't my fault. I had to lean back to see who was

coming in, and then the legs slipped.

'Oh dear,' murmured the inspector. 'Dear, oh dear. Oh dear, oh dear, oh dear.' And he scribbled something down on his notepad. I got back on my chair and we waited.

'Pay no attention to me, class. My name is Mr Bannerjee. Just pretend I'm not here.'

Mr Bannerjee went and sat near Liam. We all looked at our teacher. His face was scrunched up in pain as if he was chewing a nettle or something.

Mr Bannerjee began talking to Liam and I could just about hear Liam's answers.

'Don't know,' he said.

Mr Bannerjee went *mumble mumble* again.

'Don't know,' Liam replied.

More mumbling from the inspector.

'Don't know,' Liam sighed, while Mr Bannerjee wrote on his notepad. He glanced up at our teacher. Mr Butternut smiled back and suggested that the inspector might like to speak to Sarah Sitterbout instead.

'Why's that?' asked Mr Bannerjee.

'Because she knows about everything,' declared Hartley Tartly-Green. 'Except trains. If you want to know about trains, ask me.'

Pete nudged me with his elbow and whispered in my ear. 'I should have brought Uncle Boring along. He knows about trains, and buses, and fish and golf clubs. In fact, he knows about anything that's utterly boring.'

We watched as Mr Bannerjee moved round the classroom. He would pick on someone and then go and ask them questions. Eventually he got to our table, which Pete and I share with Mia and Erin and Sam.

'Just ignore me,' said Mr Bannerjee as he leaned over Erin's work to see what she was doing. 'Ah, I see you're drawing a jungle.'

Erin stopped dead and stared at the inspector. 'No, I'm not!' she said, pulling a disgusted face. 'I'm writing a story!'

Mr Bannerjee bent closer over Erin's book. 'That's handwriting?' he asked.

'Of course it is! Are you wearing the right glasses?'

I think I'd look good in glasses – sunglasses!

Why did the inspector keep picking on the things some of us weren't good at?

Then Sam asked a question.

'Are you wearing bifocals or varifocals?' Sam pointed at the inspector's glasses.

'Varifocals,' Mr Bannerjee told him.

'I think that's the problem,' Sam advised. 'With varifocals, there's a place on the lens where what you see is a bit blurry. Erin's handwriting is a bit scruffy, but it is possible to read it.'

Mr Bannerjee had taken off his spectacles and was staring at Sam in wonder. 'How do you know so much about reading glasses?'

'I'm a scientist and I wear glasses,' Sam pointed out. 'Scientists have to know about things like that.'

'Yes, I think they do,' smiled Mr Bannerjee, popping his glasses back on.

Sam continued. 'Also, my dad wears varifocals. He's always getting things wrong too. He fell over nothing yesterday.'

?&!$%?!!

Mr Bannerjee's smile disappeared
as quickly as if Sam had just shot
it with his anti-matter splatter gun.
'Hmmph. I'm an inspector. I don't
get things wrong,' he grunted, and he
said goodbye to everyone and left. We
all heaved a sigh of relief, even Mr
Butternut.

It didn't last long. We went outside
for break and Trouble came out
to play as well. Trouble came in

???

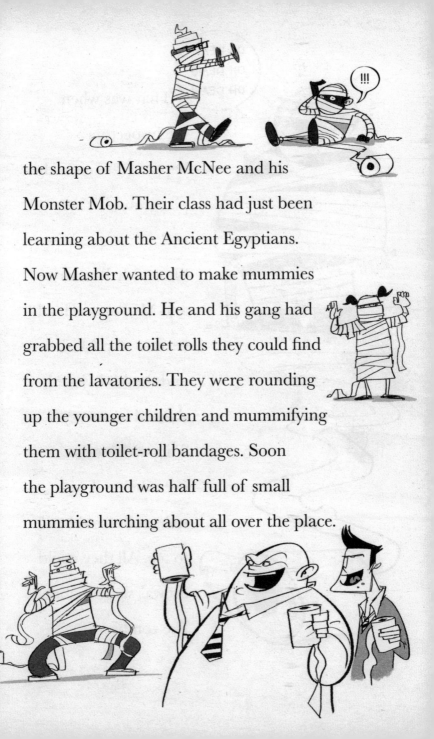

the shape of Masher McNee and his
Monster Mob. Their class had just been
learning about the Ancient Egyptians.
Now Masher wanted to make mummies
in the playground. He and his gang had
grabbed all the toilet rolls they could find
from the lavatories. They were rounding
up the younger children and mummifying
them with toilet-roll bandages. Soon
the playground was half full of small
mummies lurching about all over the place.

OH DEAR!
OH DEAR!
OH DEAR!

That was when the inspectors happened to cross the playground. There was no escape. Miss Short, Mr Bannerjee and Mr Potato Head tried to stop Masher and the Mob, but they showed no mercy. They were soon overwhelmed with toilet rolls from head to toe. All they could do was stagger about like zombies.

I had just decided it was time to go

when Miss Scratchitt and ALL the teachers came piling out of school like fighter jets on a rescue mission.

Were they cross? You bet they were. It was like watching sticks of dynamite explode all over the playground.

BANNG! BOOM!! SPLUDDD!!!
SPINNG!!!! BOOFFF!!!!!

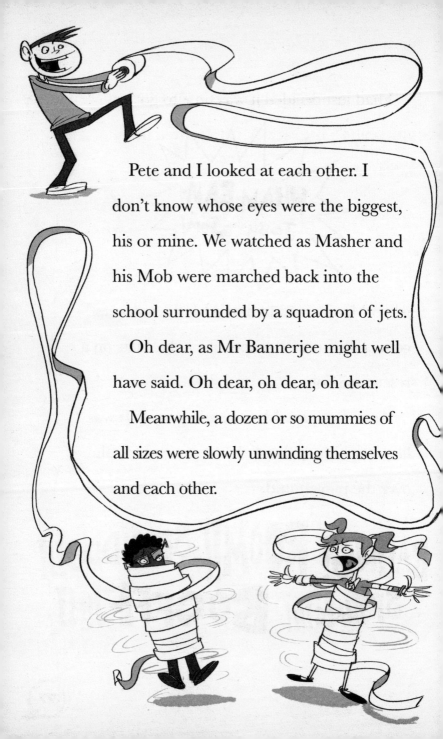

Pete and I looked at each other. I don't know whose eyes were the biggest, his or mine. We watched as Masher and his Mob were marched back into the school surrounded by a squadron of jets.

Oh dear, as Mr Bannerjee might well have said. Oh dear, oh dear, oh dear.

Meanwhile, a dozen or so mummies of all sizes were slowly unwinding themselves and each other.

When we went back to class after break, Mr Horrible Hairy Face (Mr Butternut, in other words) was waiting.

'There's been trouble in the playground,' he began, but of course we already knew, and Hartley Tartly-Green began squealing. Sometimes he sounds like a mouse who's just had all his cheese stolen.

'It was Masher and his gang and they tied everyone up with toilet roll and Miss Short almost fell over and –'

Mr Horrible Hairy Face held up a hand. 'Thank you, Hartley, we know what happened. The inspectors are NOT impressed and it will be the whole school that gets into trouble.'

'Put Masher in prison!' squeaked Hartley.

'Um, the school doesn't actually have its own dungeon, Hartley,' Mr Butternut explained.

Sam was waving his hand around. 'We could cryogenically suspend them in a state of inanimation,' he suggested.

Even Mr Butternut's beard looked surprised. 'Cryo-what?' he asked.

'Cryogenically – it means we freeze them,' Sam said cheerfully. 'It's like putting them into a deep freeze.'

'I see. I don't think we'd better do that either, Sam.'

'Oh.' Sam was disappointed, but he hadn't finished. 'Maybe we *should* try and build a time machine? Then we could go back and put everything right?'

'Let's all just get on with our work,' muttered Mr Butternut.

So we did.

Lunchtime brought even more problems. It was Chip Day.

I say make Friday Fly Day!

It's the best day of the week. Yum yum! I like chips. We all love them, even Noella Niblet, who is always moaning about everything. (Like I said, Pete and I call her The Incredible Sulk!) She happened to be sitting with us at lunch.

'My chips are shorter than yours,' she complained. 'And *your* chips are fatter. My chips aren't chippy at all.'

But before Noella could carry on, a big rumpus broke out several tables away from ours. We all turned to look. I might have known! It was Gory and Tory, the Vampire Twins.

'Hey! Those are my chips! Give them back!' someone yelled.

'You've got my chips, you chip robber!' roared someone else.

It made no difference. The Vampire Twins were flying about the lunch hall stealing chips right off people's plates. Yelling children were chasing after them. Other tables defended themselves by flicking bits of lunch at the twins. Pieces of broccoli spun through the air. Carrots rained down like crazy orange darts. Food was soon flying in all directions.

The dinner ladies stood in the middle, barking at everyone. One of them received a direct hit from a broccoli floret. *WHOPP!* It jammed in her mouth just as she was bellowing 'STO–!!'

At that moment the inspectors arrived.

They stared in shocked amazement with their

eyeballs on stalks. It was definitely time for

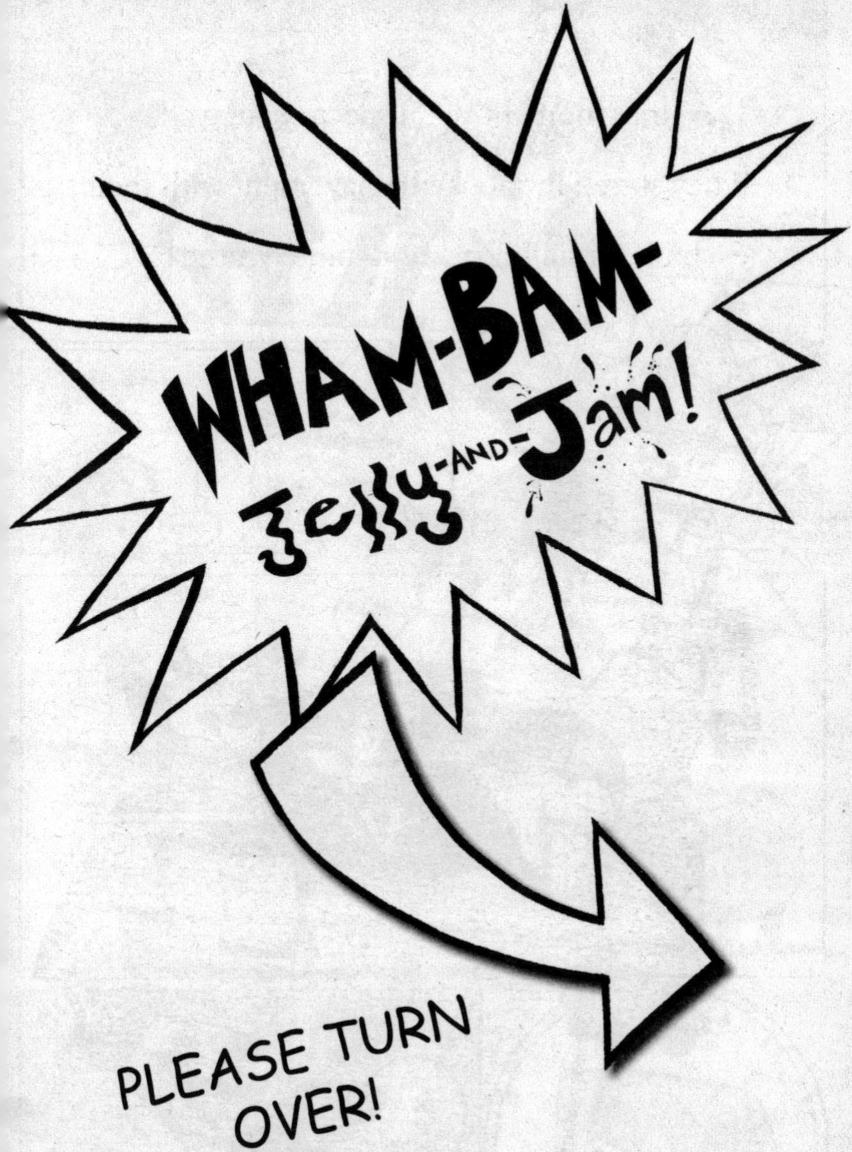


PLEASE TURN OVER!

OH DEAR, AGAIN!

I SHALL DRAW A SPECIAL WEAPON!

USE THIS!

I'VE BEEN SUCKERED!

SO HAVE I!

MUNCH! MUNCH!

WELL DONE! YOU HAVE SAVED OUR LUNCH!

If only that was what really happened. But it didn't. Mr Potato Head began bellowing, and, boy, could he bark! That Mr Potato Head could be pretty scary, if you ask me! Everyone froze. Miss Scratchitt got sent for and WE got bawled out, even though it was all the fault of the Vampire Twins. Typical.

Every class had to work in silence for the whole afternoon. It was utterly, gutterly BORING. Plus, Mr Horrible Hairy Face was in a bad mood all afternoon. When we went home, he stood at the classroom door looking grim. He gave us a strange message.

'Tomorrow morning, I want you to bring in as many cardboard boxes as you can.'

Was that mysterious? Yes, it was.

What a strange sight! The following
morning all you could see were boxes
marching into school. Some were
being pushed, some pulled and some
were over people's heads. There were
so many piled up in the classroom
that we could barely move.

'My box is the best,' boasted
Hartley Tartly-Green. 'Because my
box had a super deluxe seventy-
inch flat screen Blu-ray TV with
integrated DVD, CD player and
everything in it.'

YEAH? WELL OUR TV MAKES TOAST.

Mr Butternut laughed. 'Hey, I'd love a TV that made toast! Brilliant!'

Well, he seemed to have cheered up a bit since yesterday! Maybe it was because this would be the last day with the inspectors hanging around us like hungry zombies.

As soon as we had settled down, Mr Butternut stood up by his desk and addressed us. (I don't mean he stuck labels on us with our addresses; I mean he gave a little speech.)

'Today we are going to show the inspectors that we are a BRILLIANT class. We are going to do something very special.'

'Blow up the school?' suggested Tyson from the back, and everyone laughed.

(BAD IDEA)

'No, Tyson, not that. We are going to find out all about the Vikings. In fact, we are going TO BE Vikings.'

'But, Mr Butternut,' said Sarah Sitterbout, 'the Vikings lived a thousand years ago. They're all dead.'

Mr Butternut just smiled. 'We are going to build a time machine and go back in time to meet them.'

Sam was overjoyed. 'That was MY idea! Boop-a-loopa, super-doopa!'

That teacher of ours is pretty clever, if

you ask me. I never knew you could make a
time machine out of cardboard boxes, but
you can – AND WE DID! It took us most of
the morning and it was *MUCHO
JUMBO*! Mr Butternut told
us we all had to go through
the machine and when we
came out the other side
we would have travelled
back one thousand
years in time.

You'll never guess what we found when we came out the other side. There was a *ginormous* pile of Viking clothes, and we all dressed up. It was *FANTABULOSO*! (Except my helmet was too big and kept slipping to one side.)

Pete sniggered. 'You look about as dangerous as a hamster with a lolly, my ginger Viking pal.'

'And you will look very stupid with my lolly stuck up your nose,' I threatened. 'So there.'

That was when Mr Butternut climbed on to his desk. He waved his arms and yelled at us. Unfortunately, he had his back to our classroom door, so he didn't see Miss Short and Mr Potato Head creep inside. They stood at the back, almost out of sight.

Meanwhile, we were cheering our excited teacher.

I AM ERIK BLOODNUT, YOUR VIKING CHIEF!

'My mighty warriors! We must hold a
Thing!'

What was he going on about? What *thing*?
The only thing he was holding was a plastic
sword.

'The Vikings had special meetings called
Things. They would settle problems and
deal with criminals. Today we are holding a
Thing to decide what to do with the criminals
Masher McNee and the Vampire Twins. WE
MUST STOP THEM! Stand on your chairs if
you're with me!'

Erik Bloodnut waved his sword angrily while
we all yelled and cheered and climbed on to
our chairs.

WE COULD GET THE INSPECTORS TOO!

'Yeah! Get the inspectors! Make them walk the plank!' shouted Noella.

'That's what pirates did, not the Vikings,' Cameron told her.

'What would Vikings do, then, clever clogs?' she demanded, and Cameron shrugged.

Erik Bloodnut came to his rescue.

'The Vikings would make you walk across a room holding a red-hot piece of metal. Then they would bandage your hand.

'After a week the bandage would be taken off, and if your hand was healing you would be declared innocent, and if it wasn't you'd be guilty,' explained Erik Bloodnut.

'Sounds good to me,' shouted Tyson.

'It's a bit harsh,' Erik Bloodnut suggested. 'Especially for the inspectors. Anyhow, we are here to learn about Vikings. They would often send out raiding parties, so this is what I think we should do.'

At the back of the room the two inspectors had made for the door. They looked a bit worried. I think they thought we might suddenly give them red-hot metal rods to hold.

Erik Bloodnut divided us into two raiding parties, and with Bloodnut in the lead we crept out of the room and headed towards our targets.

The first raiding party went to the Vampire
Twins' class. They burst in, shouting like crazy,
and dragged them out, kicking and screaming.

The second raiding party, which included
Pete Lolly-Nose and myself, went to Masher
McNee's classroom. We smashed our way in,
roaring furiously, and captured Masher AND
his gang.

We took all the prisoners back to our classroom and stood over them with our swords at the ready. We made them scrub our classroom floor as a punishment, and wash our windows too. Unfortunately, the buckets of water kept getting knocked and our prisoners got pretty wet. I just can't imagine how that happened – ha ha!

That afternoon, everyone had to go to a special assembly to hear what the inspectors had to say about our school. Miss Short stood at the front.

'Things got off to a pretty bad start,' she told us. 'We were not at all impressed. But today one class showed us what this school is capable of. Mr Butternut and his children had a very inspiring history lesson. They made history come alive by time-travelling and turning their class into a group of Vikings. It was a brilliant way to learn about the past.'

To tell you the truth, Miss Short droned on and on until half the reception children were falling asleep, and my friend Pete was doing such big yawns I thought he might swallow a hippo. Good thing there wasn't a hippo wandering around in the hall.

So everything was all right in the end.

Was that *stupendo*? It certainly was!

Zombies? Vikings?
Hippos? I shall never
understand humans!

That is the noise my dad makes when he's painting and he's just splattered a large dollop of paint on his shoe, or the floor, or the table, or the lampshade, or the TV, or his head, or the cat (good thing we don't have one!), or really anywhere at all.

That's because my dad is MR SLOPPY-MESS when he's doing the decorating. In fact, last year he was painting the bathroom and he actually managed to put his WHOLE FOOT in the paint tub. He might as well fill the bath with paint, jump in and get the job done properly.

Dad is decorating Abbie's bedroom, and that means there's a BIG *PROBLEMO*! Where is Abbie sleeping while her bedroom (and my dad) are covered in wet paint? I will tell you. She's sleeping on a folding bed in my room! Is that *AAAAAARGH!* or not? It is definitely double, triple, quadruple

Poor Casper!

# AAARRRGGGHHH!

Would you like to share your bedroom with your fourteen-year-old big sis? I DON'T THINK SO! She is a pea-brained stinky pimple. So, as you can tell, basically we are AT WAR, and now the stinky pimple is sleeping IN MY BEDROOM! How bad is that? It's

# THIS BAD!!!

What's more, she isn't alone. She has brought with her –

LIPSTICK

COMB

EYELASHES

MUMMY?

HAIR SPRAY

hair Spray

BRUSH

TEETH

I don't know how those teeth
got there. They look like Great-
Grannie's falsies to me, so why
has my sister got Gee-Gee's teeth?
It's a MYSTERY waiting to be
solved by the world's greatest
detective, Casper Jenkinson.

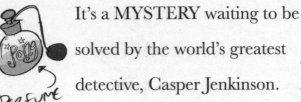

PERFUME

KNICKERS

(That's me!) What is more, I know the answer, and I will tell you what it is. Those teeth are there because my sister is MISS GIGANTIC NINCOMPOOPLE-PERSON! (As you can see from my drawing of her.)

Anyhow, big sis has turned my bedroom into a jumble sale. There's hardly any space to breathe – and, if you do manage to breathe,

you immediately DROWN in the

DEADLY POISONOUS AROMA of

Something tells me Casper is exaggerating.

Abbie's smelly clothes and perfumes. I

have to wear my swimming goggles and

snorkel.

When Pete came round to see me he

was aghast.

'You're sharing your room with a

GIRL!' he said, as if I didn't know.

'Yes, I am, O Tall and Enormously

Footed Person. I am in the Deepest

Depths of Despair.'

Pete pulled a face. 'Can't you get rid

of her?

'Dad says it will only be for three

nights.'

Pete was horrified. 'Three nights! But that's like a whole YEAR!' And he threw himself on to Abbie's folding bed.

I just about managed to lever open the bed so that Pete could crawl out. He fell to the floor, gasping for breath.

'Perhaps I should have warned you not to sit on the folding bed too hard,' I told him.

'Casper,' he began, because that's my name, 'you have got a man-eating bed in your room. It should be in a zoo, with a big warning notice.'

'Pete,' I answered, because that's *his* name, 'that bed is going to stay right here. Do you know why? Because with a bit of luck it might eat Abbie.'

We both thought that was so funny
Pete went into hysterics and fell back
down on the bed.

KERRDANNG!

Oh no! I don't
believe it!

Some people never learn.

So there we are. I have to tell you it
is very strange sleeping with a weird
alien in your room. Abbie made bizarre
noises all night long. I hardly got a wink
of sleep. She kept mumbling to herself.

I couldn't hear most of what she said, but every so often she would shout out something like 'HIPPOS!' or 'UMBRELLA!'. And once she suddenly sat up and yelled, 'STOP THE TALKING CAKE!'

By the time morning came I was so tired I could barely stand. I told Mum and Dad. I pleaded with them.

'Abbie kept me awake all night. Can she PLEASE sleep somewhere else?'

'There isn't anywhere else for her to sleep, Casper,' Dad explained. 'I'm sorry. You'll just have to put up with it. It's only for two more nights.'

'Can't you paint the bedroom faster?' I suggested.

Dad grunted. 'Casper, I am not a superhero. I have to go to work as well as get the decorating done. I'm painting as fast as I can.'

Poor Dad. He did look a bit worn out, doing two jobs. It was all too depressing. I decided to go round to Pete's house. (That made a change – he usually comes round to mine.)

The moment his front door opened, Pete tried to whisk me upstairs to his room so we could talk in private. 'Uncle Boring is here,' he muttered.

Uncle Boring isn't just boring – he's SO BORING he's probably a zombie.

Uncle Boring likes buses and ties and he says things like: 'Oh, look, there's a Vauxhall Cavalier, the 1981 model. I haven't seen one of those since, hmmmm, 1981.'

Which, as you can tell, is about as exciting as listening to a jellyfish playing the trumpet. So that is why we always try to AVOID him.

We failed. Uncle Boring caught us just as we were tippety-toeing halfway up the stairs.

'Hello, boys!' he boomed. 'What are you up to?'

'We're going to my room to do our homework,' Pete answered.

'Anything I can help with?' asked Uncle Boring, stroking his tie. 'I was top of my class when I was at school.'

'It's . . . um . . .' stumbled Pete. He nudged me desperately. 'Tell me what it is we have to do again, Casper?'

'Oh, er, yes. We have to . . . erm . . . paint a . . . and then we need to . . . erm . . . yes, and it's . . . er . . . paint . . . and hmmm – difficult, really.'

'Yes, difficult,' Pete repeated. 'Definitely. Very.'

Uncle Boring beamed at us. 'I shall leave you to it, then. You can show me later.' He disappeared back into the front room and we breathed a sigh of relief.

Once we were safely shut inside Pete's bedroom, he looked at me steadily. 'Spill the beans.'

WHAT'S UP, MY KNOBBLY GINGER TWIGLET?

I told him about the previous night.

'Hippos and talking cake?' he repeated.

'Your sister needs a psychia-thingummy-bob.'

'Psychiatrist?' I suggested.

'Definitely one of those,' Pete nodded.

'Maybe even three or four.'

THERE'S NO HOPE FOR THIS ONE . . .

'I've got to get Abbie out of my room.'

'Exactly. But she can't leave until your dad finishes painting HER room.'

'Big *problemo*,' I murmured.

'Big *problemo*,' Pete echoed. 'Unless –

UNLESS – the painting gets done a lot more quickly!'

'How? Mum's baking cakes by the million, as usual, and Dad's at work.'

'*We* paint it,' Pete said. 'We paint the room ourselves. You and me.'

We looked at each other. We could almost SEE each other's brains whizzing round. That friend of mine is a genius – even if he does look like a twit.

I can feel trouble coming...

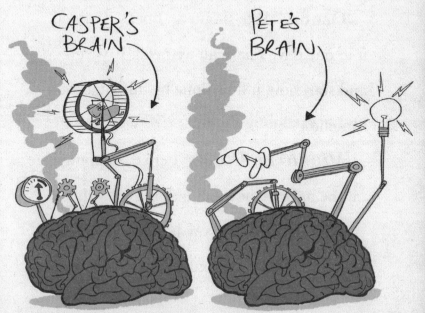

CASPER'S BRAIN

PETE'S BRAIN

The more we thought about it, the more it made sense. The paint was there in the bedroom, waiting for us. All we had to do was get on with it. Not only that, it would help my dad and he would be utterly-chuckley PLEASED! So, if it took one person three days to paint the room, then surely it would take two people, er . . . um . . . er . . .

'One day!' Pete shouted. 'I bet we can do it in one day! That's all we need. If we go and start now, it'll be done by this afternoon sometime.'

'*MUCHO FABULOSO!*' I cried, slapping Pete on the back. 'Come on, let's get on with it!'

We dashed back to my house and whizzed upstairs. Abbie had gone off to spend the day with her best friend, Shashi. Mum was in the kitchen, up to her ears making cupcakes and flapjacks for a big party. (It's her job – nice one! Yum yum!) Dad was working. Perfect.

We nipped into Abbie's room. Dad had cleared most of the furniture out. The paint tins and brushes were piled in one corner. Pete and I seized the two big brushes and got to work.

It's funny how sloppy paint can be. And another thing – after you've been painting for five minutes, your fingers and wrist start to ache because of all that brush-gripping you've been doing.

I'M EXHAUSTED!

'There's got to be a faster method than this,' said Pete. 'I think Dad uses a roller, but I don't know where he's put it. Wait a moment. I'm getting an idea. Come with me.'

Paint

I hurtled into my room and dived into the wardrobe. Somewhere I had – AHA! FOUND THEM!

'Will it work?' Pete asked.

'Of course. Why wouldn't it?'

No, don't do it! This is a BAD idea!

'Er . . . because I'm just not sure about it.'

'Don't be such a wuss.'

'I'm not a wuss.'

'In that case let's go and load up!' I cried.

I can tell you, I reckoned I was pretty

stunningly clever to come up with that idea.
In fact, it just about made me a GENIUS!
So now we were both geniuses. *Marvelloso!*

   We went back to Abbie's room and
carefully filled up. 'You take that wall and I'll
do this one. Ready?'

   'Ready!'

   'In that case, LET'S PAINT THIS
ROOM! YAY!'

We kept going until we'd covered every little bit of the room. Guess how long it took us? Ten minutes. TEN MINUTES to paint an entire bedroom! Was that a world record, or what? I will tell you. It was the most superest-duperest world record in the history of world records.

Pete and I stepped back into the middle of the room and looked at our handiwork. Paint was slurping down every wall and slowly trickling on to the floor, piling up round the edges of the room.

· We heard loud footsteps on the stairs
and looked at each other desperately.
Where can you hide in a completely
empty room? Nowhere. So we hid there.

The door swung open and Mum
walked in.

Do you know what someone looks like
when they have gone into deep DEEP
SHOCK? They look like this.

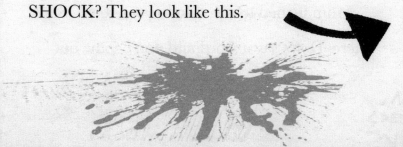

MY MUM

(SILENT SCREAM OF HORROR!)

Mum stared at Pete, her eyes like frozen peas. (I don't mean they were green – just that she was giving him an ICY look.)

'OK, I'm going,' Pete said quickly, and he slid out of the room, raced downstairs (leaving wet paint prints all the way down) and left.

Mum turned to me. 'Go to your room. Stay there. Don't say a word and don't come out.'

Uh-oh. Trouble.

When Dad came home, Mum sent him upstairs to inspect the damage. Well, actually all he had to do was follow the trail of paint prints Pete had left behind. Some of them were still wet. I waited for the KER-BOOM of anger. I waited and waited, getting more and more nervous. Finally, the bedroom door opened and Dad poked his head round the corner.

CASPER . . .

His voice was deadly quiet, but his eyes were burning like nuclear explosions. 'I would just like to say that when you grow up, I hope you have LOTS and LOTS of children who are just like YOU!' He pulled the door shut and left.

Silence.

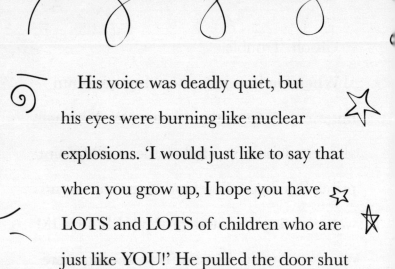

I'm an adult and even I don't understand!

Huh! What was that supposed to mean? I was in the dark, and I don't mean the light had gone out. I mean I didn't understand my dad. I guess that's because he's an adult.

Anyhow, what Pete and I did to

Abbie's room made the painting take even longer – and I ended up having to share my bedroom with big sis for almost a whole week and things became mega strange and peculiar.

'You can take that as your punishment for interfering,' said Dad. Which was pretty unfair, if you ask me. I was only trying to help. So I had all those extra nights with Abbie muttering in her sleep and saying stuff like 'PUT A SOCK IN IT!' and 'THE LEMON MERINGUE LIED!' And then, on the third night, she actually got up and started wandering about, but she was STILL ASLEEP! Big sis was sleepwalking!

I went and woke Mum and Dad. They weren't very pleased, I can tell you, but they got up and we followed Abbie all the way downstairs. She went into the kitchen, opened the fridge, took out a bottle of milk, poured half of it on the floor, put the milk back, shut the fridge, went back to bed, lay down and began to snore.

Zzzzzzzz

Is my sister strange, or what? She is more than strange. She is a ZOMBIE! In fact, she is The Zombie That Snores!

The next day Mum and Dad took Abbie to the health centre and Doctor Chandra said there was nothing wrong with her. What! Nothing wrong with Abbie? Huh! I could have told

PIGGY EYES

PEA BRAIN

TUNNEL NOSE

COCKTAIL SAUSAGES

Doctor Chandra at least a hundred things that were wrong with her, like, for example, her nose. That's all wrong for starters. Then there're her piggy eyes, and her elbows that keep sticking everywhere, and her brain – what there is of it – they're all TOTALLY wrong. Plus, she's got toes that look like cocktail sausages and a stupid, stupid voice that goes '*weeny weeny weeny*' until you want to strangle her.

'She's just a normal girl,' said Doctor Chandra. 'Teenagers, especially girls, sometimes sleepwalk. She'll grow out of it. In the meantime, keep an eye on her. It's important not to wake her up. Gently lead her to bed and she'll go back to sleep.'

'But what causes it?' asked Dad.

'Oh, just being a teenager,' smiled the doctor. 'And, of course, stress doesn't help.'

When she got home, Abbie looked at me and a smile crept across her face like a snake – a poisonous one.

STOP STRESSING ME, LITTLE BRO!

I was never so stressed in my life as when I heard that! Abbie kept laughing to herself for the rest of the day. I bet she's planning something.

So the next night comes and what does Abbie do? She goes sleepwalking again and Mum and Dad and I follow her. First she goes across to Mum and Dad's bedroom and sits in front of the mirror. Then she gets up and comes across to me and takes me by the hand. I try to pull away, but Dad says not to.

'We mustn't wake her,' he whispered. 'Go with her!'

Casper's in big trouble now!

Abbie pulls me across to the mirror and sits me down in front of it. Her eyes are staring into space and I'm thinking, *I am in the hands of a zombie! Hellppp!*

Then Abbie starts picking things up. She gets Mum's make-up. She's got the mascara and she's trying to put it on my lips. She must think it's lipstick. Now she's painting my lips with mascara. She takes the lipstick and draws round my eyes. She colours my eyebrows with blue eyeliner. I want to get away, but Mum and Dad keep whispering at me.

'Keep still. You mustn't wake her. Stop wriggling. It's OK, you look fine.'

*I LOOK FINE?! I'VE GOT BLACK LIPS, BLUE EYEBROWS AND RED LIPSTICK EYELINER!!! YOU CALL THAT FINE?!*

It's definitely time to be a superhero and go

WHAM-BAM-
Jelly -AND- Jam!

PLEASE TURN
OVER!

Sadly, it wasn't quite like that. As soon
as Abbie finished painting my face, she
sleepwalked to her camera and took a
photograph of me! Huh! Finally, she stomped
back to my bedroom, settled in bed and went
off to sleep, snoring louder than ever. She had
a big grin on her face too, which was VERY
FISHY, if you ask me. Hmmmm. Detective
Inspector Casper was highly suspicious.

First thing next morning, Abbie took her camera
to her computer and called me over.

'Hey, Casper, you should see this. Look.'

I went across and there it was – a great big
photo of me wearing all that stupid make-up and
pulling a disgusted face. Abbie was in hysterics.

148

'It's you!' she kept shouting. 'The mad
baboon! It's you! I'm going to put you on
Facebook!'

Oh yeah, ha very ha ha, I don't think.

But Abbie thought it was SO funny, she completely forgot herself and, guess what, she threw herself down on the folding bed!

Did I laugh then? Yes I did, but not until I had grabbed her camera and snapped Completely Useless Girl being snapped up by the bed. *FABULOSO!* Then I HOWLED like a hyena! Hurr hurr hurr! I love a happy ending!

I'm so glad I don't have any brothers or sisters!

# Ask Jeremy

**Of all the books you have written, which one is your favourite?**

I loved writing both **KRAZY KOW SAVES THE WORLD – WELL, ALMOST** and **STUFF**, my first book for teenagers. Both these made me laugh out loud while I was writing and I was pleased with the overall result in each case. I also love writing the stories about Nicholas and his daft family – **MY DAD**, **MY MUM**, **MY BROTHER** and so on.

**If you couldn't be a writer what would you be?**

Well, I'd be pretty fed up for a start, because writing was the one thing I knew I wanted to do from the age of nine onward. But if I DID have to do something else, I would love to be either an accomplished pianist or an artist of some sort. Music and art have played a big part in my whole life and I would love to be involved in them in some way.

**What's the best thing about writing stories?**

Oh dear – so many things to say here! Getting paid for making things up is pretty high on the list! It's also something you do on your own, inside your own head – nobody can interfere with that. The only boss you have is yourself. And you are creating something that nobody else has made before you. I also love making my readers laugh and want to read more and more.

**Did you ever have a nightmare teacher?**
**(And who was your best ever?)**

My nightmare at primary school was Mrs Chappell, long since dead. I knew her secret – she was not actually human. She was a Tyrannosaurus rex in disguise. She taught me for two years when I was in Y5 and Y6, and we didn't like each other at all. My best ever was when I was in Y3 and Y4. Her name was Miss Cox, and she was the one who first encouraged me to write stories. She was brilliant. Sadly, she is long dead too.

**When you were a kid you used to play kiss-chase. Did you always do the chasing or did anyone ever chase you?!**

I usually did the chasing, but when I got chased, I didn't bother to run very fast! Maybe I shouldn't admit to that! We didn't play kiss-chase at school – it was usually played during holidays. If we had tried playing it at school we would have been in serious trouble. Mind you, I seemed to spend most of my time in trouble of one sort or another, so maybe it wouldn't have mattered that much.

# It all started with a Scarecrow.

## Puffin is seventy years old.

Sounds ancient, doesn't it? But Puffin has never been
so lively. We're always on the lookout for the next big
idea, which is how it began all those years ago.

Penguin Books was a big idea from the mind of
a man called Allen Lane, who in 1935 invented
the quality paperback and changed the world.

**And from great Penguins, great Puffins grew,
changing the face of children's books forever.**

The first four Puffin Picture Books were hatched in 1940 and the
first Puffin story book featured a man with broomstick arms called
Worzel Gummidge. In 1967 Kaye Webb, Puffin Editor, started the
Puffin Club, promising to **'make children into readers'**.
She kept that promise and over 200,000 children became
devoted Puffineers through their quarterly instalments of
*Puffin Post*, which is now back for a new generation.

Many years from now, we hope you'll look back and
remember Puffin with a smile. **No matter what your age
or what you're into, there's a Puffin for everyone.**
The possibilities are endless, but one thing is for sure:
whether it's a picture book or a paperback, a sticker book
or a hardback, **if it's got that little Puffin
on it – it's bound to be good.**